An ancient spell, 140 tortoises, and a little bit of magic . . .

Mr. Hoppy is in love with his neighbor, Mrs. Silver; but she is in love with someone else—Alfie, her pet tortoise. With all her attention focused on Alfie, Mrs. Silver doesn't even know Mr. Hoppy is alive. And Mr. Hoppy is too shy to even ask Mrs. Silver over for tea. Then one day Mr. Hoppy comes up with a brilliant idea to get Mrs. Silver's attention. If Mr. Hoppy's plan works, Mrs. Silver will certainly fall in love with him. After all, everyone knows the way to a woman's heart is through her tortoise.

Puffin Books by Roald Dahl

ROALD DAHL
ESIO TROT

Illustrated by Quentin Blake

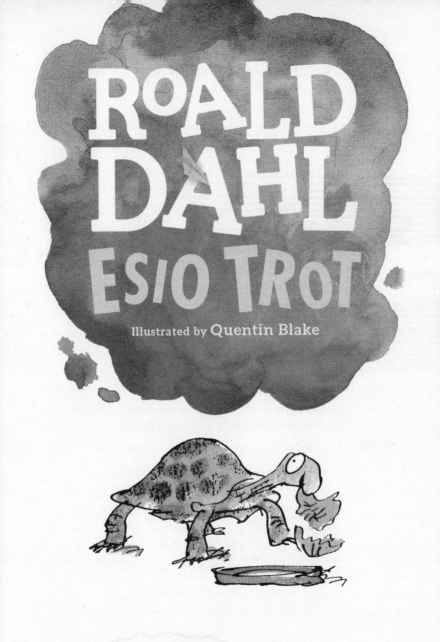

PUFFIN BOOKS

to Clover and Luke

PUFFIN BOOKS
An imprint of Penguin Random House LLC
375 Hudson Street
New York, New York 10014

First published in Great Britain by Jonathan Cape Ltd, 1990
First published in the United States of America by Viking Penguin,
a division of Penguin Books USA Inc., 1990
Published by Puffin Books, 1992
Reissued by Puffin Books, 1999, 2007
This edition reissued by Puffin Books, an imprint of
Penguin Young Readers Group, 2009, 2013

Text copyright © 1990 by Roald Dahl
Illustrations copyright © 1990 by Quentin Blake

THE LIBRARY OF CONGRESS HAS CATALOGED THE PREVIOUS PUFFIN BOOKS EDITION AS FOLLOWS:
Dahl, Roald
Esio Trot / by Roald Dahl; illustrated by Quentin Blake
p. cm.
Summary: Shy Mr. Hoppy devises a plan to win the heart of his true love
by teaching her a spell to make her tortoise grow bigger.
ISBN 978-0-14-036099-8 [1. Turtles—Fiction. 2. Size—Fiction. 3. Magic—Fiction.]
I. Blake, Quentin, ill. II. Title.
PZ7.D1515Es 1992 [Fic] —dc20 92-16931

This edition ISBN 978-0-14-241382-1

Printed in the United States of America

Within a week, Matilda had finished *Great Expectations* which in that edition contained four hundred and eleven pages. "I loved it," she said to Mrs Phelps. "Has Mr Dickens written any others?"

"A great number," said the astounded Mrs Phelps. "Shall I choose you another?"

Over the next six months, under Mrs Phelps's

watchful and compassionate eye, Matilda read the following books:

Nicholas Nickleby by Charles Dickens
Oliver Twist by Charles Dickens
Jane Eyre by Charlotte Brontë
Pride and Prejudice by Jane Austen
Tess of the D'Urbervilles by Thomas Hardy
Gone to Earth by Mary Webb
Kim by Rudyard Kipling
The Invisible Man by H. G. Wells
The Old Man and the Sea by Ernest Hemingway
The Sound and the Fury by William Faulkner
The Grapes of Wrath by John Steinbeck
The Good Companions by J. B. Priestley
Brighton Rock by Graham Greene
Animal Farm by George Orwell

It was a formidable list and by now Mrs Phelps was filled with wonder and excitement, but it was probably a good thing that she did not allow herself to be completely carried away by it all. Almost anyone else witnessing the achievements of this small child would have been tempted to make a great fuss and shout the news all over the village and beyond, but not so Mrs Phelps. She was someone who minded her own business and had long since discovered it was seldom worth while to interfere with other people's children.

"Mr Hemingway says a lot of things I don't understand," Matilda said to her. "Especially about men and women. But I loved it all the same. The way he tells it I feel I am right there on the spot watching it all happen."

"A fine writer will always make you feel that," Mrs Phelps said. "And don't worry about the bits you can't understand. Sit back and allow the words to wash around you, like music."

"I will, I will."

"Did you know", Mrs Phelps said, "that public libraries like this allow you to borrow books and take them home?"

"I didn't know that," Matilda said. "Could *I* do it?"

"Of course," Mrs Phelps said. "When you have chosen the book you want, bring it to me so I can make a note of it and it's yours for two weeks. You can take more than one if you wish."

From then on, Matilda would visit the library only once a week in order to take out new books and return the old ones. Her own small bedroom now became her reading-room and there she would sit and read most afternoons, often with a mug of hot chocolate beside her. She was not quite tall enough to reach things around the kitchen, but she kept a small box in the outhouse which she brought in and stood on in order to get whatever she wanted. Mostly it was hot chocolate she made, warming the milk in a saucepan on the stove before mixing it. Occasionally she made Bovril or Ovaltine. It was pleasant to take a hot drink up to her room and have it beside her as she sat in her silent room reading in the empty house in the afternoons. The books transported her into new worlds and introduced her to amazing people who lived exciting lives. She went on olden-day sailing ships with Joseph Conrad. She went to Africa with Ernest Hemingway and to India with Rudyard Kipling. She travelled all over the world while sitting in her little room in an English village.

STORIES ARE GOOD FOR YOU.

Roald Dahl said,
*"If you have good thoughts, they will shine
out of your face like sunbeams and you
will always look lovely."*

We believe in doing good things.
That's why 10 percent of all Roald Dahl income*
goes to our charity partners. We have supported
causes including: specialist children's nurses, grants for
families in need, and educational outreach programs.
Thank you for helping us to sustain this vital work.

Find out more at roalddahl.com

The Roald Dahl Charitable Trust is a registered UK charity (no. 1119330).
* All author payments and royalty income net of third-party commissions.

Author's Note

Some years ago, when my own children were small, we usually kept a tortoise or two in the garden. In those days, a pet tortoise was a common sight crawling about on the family lawn or in the backyard. You could buy them quite cheaply in any pet shop and they were probably the least troublesome of all childhood pets, and quite harmless.

Tortoises used to be brought into England by the thousand, packed in crates, and they came mostly from North Africa. But not many years ago a law was passed that made it illegal to bring any tortoises into the country. This was not done to protect us. The little tortoise was not a danger to anybody. It was done purely out of kindness to the tortoise itself. You see, the traders who brought them in used to cram hundreds of them tightly into the packing-crates without food or water and in such horrible conditions that a great many of them always died on the sea journey over. So rather than allow this cruelty to go on, the Government stopped the whole business.

The things you are going to read about in this story all happened in the days when anyone could go out and buy a nice little tortoise from a pet shop.

ESIO TROT

Mr Hoppy lived in a small flat high up in a tall concrete building. He lived alone. He had always been a lonely man and now that he was retired from work he was more lonely than ever.

There were two loves in Mr Hoppy's life. One was the flowers he grew on his balcony. They grew in pots and tubs and baskets, and in summer the little balcony became a riot of colour.

Mr Hoppy's second love was a secret he kept entirely to himself.

The balcony immediately below Mr Hoppy's jutted out a good bit further from the building than his own, so Mr Hoppy always had a fine view of what was going on down there. This balcony belonged to an attractive middle-aged lady called Mrs Silver. Mrs Silver was a widow who also lived alone. And although she didn't know it, it was she who was the object of Mr Hoppy's secret love. He had loved her from his balcony for many years, but he was a very shy man and he had never been able to bring himself to give her even the smallest hint of his love.

Every morning, Mr Hoppy and Mrs Silver exchanged polite conversation, the one looking down from above, the other looking up, but that was as far as it ever went. The distance between their balconies might not have been more than a few yards, but to Mr Hoppy it seemed like a million miles. He longed to invite Mrs Silver up for a cup of tea and a biscuit, but every time he was about to form the words on his lips, his courage failed him. As I said, he was a very very shy man.

Oh, if only, he kept telling himself, if only he could do something tremendous like saving her life or rescuing her from a gang of armed thugs, if only he could perform some great feat that would make him a hero in her eyes. If only...

The trouble with Mrs Silver was that she gave all her love to somebody else, and that somebody was a small tortoise called Alfie. Every day, when Mr Hoppy looked over his balcony and saw Mrs Silver whispering endearments to Alfie and stroking his shell, he felt absurdly jealous. He wouldn't even have minded becoming a tortoise himself if it meant Mrs Silver stroking his shell each morning and whispering endearments to him.

Alfie had been with Mrs Silver for years and he lived on her balcony summer and winter. Planks had been placed around the sides of the balcony so that Alfie could walk about without toppling over the edge, and in one corner there was a little house into which Alfie would crawl every night to keep warm.

When the colder weather came along in November, Mrs Silver would fill Alfie's house

with dry hay, and the tortoise would crawl in
there and bury himself deep under the hay and
go to sleep for months on end without food or
water. This is called hibernating.

In early spring, when Alfie felt the warmer
weather through his shell, he would wake up
and crawl very slowly out of his house onto the
balcony. And Mrs Silver would clap her hands
with joy and cry out, "Welcome back, my
darling one! Oh, how I have missed you!"

It was at times like these that Mr Hoppy
wished more than ever that he could change
places with Alfie and become a tortoise.

Now we come to a certain bright
morning in May when something
happened that changed and indeed
electrified Mr Hoppy's life. He was
leaning over his balcony rail watching
Mrs Silver serving Alfie his breakfast.

"Here's the heart of the lettuce for you,
my lovely," she was saying. "And here's a
slice of fresh tomato and a piece of crispy
celery."

"Good morning, Mrs Silver," Mr Hoppy
said. "Alfie's looking well this morning."

"Isn't he gorgeous!" Mrs Silver said, looking
up and beaming at him.

"Absolutely gorgeous," Mr Hoppy said, not
meaning it. And now, as he looked down at Mrs
Silver's smiling face gazing up into his own, he
thought for the thousandth time how pretty she
was, how sweet and gentle and full of kindness,
and his heart ached with love.

"I do so wish he would *grow* a little faster," Mrs Silver was saying. "Every spring, when he wakes up from his winter sleep, I weigh him on the kitchen scales. And do you know that in all the eleven years I've had him he's not gained more than *three ounces*! That's almost *nothing*!"

"What does he weigh now?" Mr Hoppy asked her.

"Just thirteen ounces," Mrs Silver answered. "About as much as a grapefruit."

"Yes, well, tortoises are very slow growers," Mr Hoppy said solemnly. "But they can live for a hundred years."

"I know that," Mrs Silver said. "But I do so wish he would grow just a little bit bigger. He's such a tiny wee fellow."

"He seems just fine as he is," Mr Hoppy said.

"No, he's *not* just fine!" Mrs Silver cried. "Try

to think how miserable it must make him feel to be so titchy! Everyone wants to grow up."

"You really *would* love him to grow bigger, wouldn't you?" Mr Hoppy said, and even as he said it his mind suddenly went *click* and an amazing idea came rushing into his head.

"Of course I would!" Mrs Silver cried. "I'd give *anything* to make it happen! Why, I've seen pictures of giant tortoises that are so huge people can ride on their backs! If Alfie were to see those he'd turn green with envy!"

Mr Hoppy's mind was spinning like a fly-wheel. Here, surely, was his big chance! Grab it, he told himself. Grab it quick!

"Mrs Silver," he said. "I do actually happen to know how to make tortoises grow faster, if that's really what you want."

"You do?" she cried. "Oh, please tell me! Am I feeding him the wrong things?"

"I worked in North Africa once," Mr Hoppy said. "That's where all these tortoises in England come from, and a bedouin tribesman told me the secret."

"Tell me!" cried Mrs Silver. "I beg you to tell me, Mr Hoppy! I'll be your slave for life."

When he heard the words *your slave for life*, a little shiver of excitement swept through Mr Hoppy. "Wait there," he said. "I'll have to go in and write something down for you."

In a couple of minutes Mr Hoppy was back on the balcony with a sheet of paper in his hand. "I'm going to lower it to you on a bit of string," he said, "or it might blow away. Here it comes."

Mrs Silver caught the paper and held it up in front of her. This is what she read:

ESIO TROT, ESIO TROT,
TEG REGGIB REGGIB!
EMOC NO, ESIO TROT,
WORG PU, FFUP PU, TOOHS PU!
GNIRPS PU, WOLB PU, LLEWS PU!
EGROG! ELZZUG! FFUTS! PLUG!
TUP NO TAF, ESIO TROT, TUP NO TAF!
TEG NO, TEG NO! ELBBOG DOOF!

"What *does* it mean?" she asked. "Is it another language?"

"It's tortoise language," Mr Hoppy said. "Tortoises are very backward creatures. Therefore they can only understand words that are written backwards. That's obvious, isn't it?"

"I suppose so," Mrs Silver said, bewildered.

"Esio trot is simply tortoise spelled backwards," Mr Hoppy said. "Look at it."

"So it is," Mrs Silver said.

"The other words are spelled backwards, too," Mr Hoppy said. "If you turn them round into human language, they simply say:

TORTOISE, TORTOISE,
GET BIGGER BIGGER!
COME ON, TORTOISE,
GROW UP, PUFF UP, SHOOT UP!
SPRING UP, BLOW UP, SWELL UP!
GORGE! GUZZLE! STUFF! GULP!
PUT ON FAT, TORTOISE, PUT ON FAT!
GET ON, GET ON! GOBBLE FOOD!"

Mrs Silver examined the magic words on the paper more closely. "I guess you're right," she said. "How clever. But there's an awful lot of poos in it. Are they something special?"

"Poo is a very strong word in any language," Mr Hoppy said, "especially with tortoises. Now what you have to do, Mrs Silver, is hold Alfie up to your face and whisper these words to him three times a day, morning, noon and night. Let me hear you practice them."

Very slowly and stumbling a little over the strange words, Mrs Silver read the whole message out loud in tortoise language.

"Not bad," Mr Hoppy said. "But try to get a little more expression into it when you say it to Alfie. If you do it properly I'll bet you anything you like that in a few months' time he'll be twice as big as he is now."

"I'll try it," Mrs Silver said. "I'll try anything. Of course I will. But I can't believe it'll work."

"You wait and see," Mr Hoppy said, smiling at her.

Back in his flat, Mr Hoppy was simply quiv-
ering all over with excitement. *Your slave for life*,
he kept repeating to himself. What bliss!

But there was a lot of work to be done before
that happened.

The only furniture in Mr Hoppy's small living room was a table and two chairs. These he moved into his bedroom. Then he went out and bought a sheet of thick canvas and spread it over the entire living room floor to protect his carpet.

Next, he got out the telephone book and wrote down the address of every pet shop in the city. There were fourteen of them altogether.

It took him two days to visit each pet shop and choose his tortoises. He wanted a great many, at least one hundred, perhaps more. And he had to choose them very carefully.

To you and me there is not much difference between one tortoise and another. They differ only in their size and in the colour of their shells. Alfie had a darkish shell, so Mr Hoppy chose only the darker-shelled tortoises for his great collection.

Size, of course, was everything. Mr Hoppy chose all sorts of different sizes, some weighing only slightly more than Alfie's thirteen ounces, others a great deal more, but he didn't want any that weighed less.

"Feed them cabbage leaves," the pet shop owners told him. "That's all they'll need. And a bowl of water."

When he had finished, Mr Hoppy, in his enthusiasm, had bought no less than one hundred and forty tortoises and he carried them home in baskets, ten or fifteen at a time. He had to make a lot of trips and he was quite exhausted at the end of it all, but it was worth it. Boy, was it worth it! And what an amazing sight his living room was when they were all in there together! The floor was swarming with tortoises of different sizes, some walking slowly about and exploring, some munching cabbage leaves, others drinking water from a big shallow dish. They made just the faintest rustling sound as they moved over the canvas sheet, but that was all. Mr Hoppy had to pick his way carefully on his toes between this moving sea of brown shells whenever he walked across the room. But enough of that. He must get on with the job.

Before he retired Mr Hoppy had been a
mechanic in a bus-garage. And now he went
back to his old place of work and asked his mates
if he might use his old bench for an hour or two.

What he had to do now was to make
something that would reach down from his own
balcony to Mrs Silver's balcony and pick up a
tortoise. This was not difficult for a mechanic
like Mr Hoppy.

First he made two metal claws or fingers, and these he attached to the end of a long metal tube. He ran two stiff wires down inside the tube and connected them to the metal claws in such a way that when you pulled the wires, the claws closed, and when you pushed them, the claws opened. The wires were joined to a handle at the other end of the tube. It was all very simple.

Mr Hoppy was ready to begin.

Mrs Silver had a part-time job. She worked from noon until five o'clock every weekday afternoon in a shop that sold newspapers and sweets. That made things a lot easier for Mr Hoppy.

So on that first exciting afternoon, after he had made sure that Mrs Silver had gone to work, Mr Hoppy went out onto his balcony armed with his long metal pole. He called this his tortoise-catcher. He leaned over the balcony railings and lowered the pole down onto Mrs Silver's balcony below. Alfie was basking in the pale sunlight over to one side.

"Hello Alfie," Mr Hoppy said. "You are about to go for a little ride."

He wiggled the tortoise-catcher till it was right above Alfie. He pushed the hand-lever so that the claws opened wide. Then he lowered the two claws neatly over Alfie's shell and pulled the lever. The claws closed tightly over the shell like two fingers of a hand. He hauled Alfie up on to his own balcony. It was easy.

Mr Hoppy weighed Alfie on his own kitchen scales just to make sure that Mrs Silver's figure of thirteen ounces was correct. It was.

Now, holding Alfie in one hand, he picked his way carefully through his huge collection of tortoises to find one that first of all had the same colour shell as Alfie's and secondly weighed *exactly two ounces more*.

Two ounces is not much. It is less than a smallish hen's egg weighs. But you see, the important thing in Mr Hoppy's plan was to make sure that the new tortoise was bigger than Alfie but only a *tiny bit* bigger. The difference had to be so small that Mrs Silver wouldn't notice it.

From his vast collection, it was not difficult for Mr Hoppy to find just the tortoise he wanted. He wanted one that weighed fifteen ounces exactly on his kitchen scales, no more and no less. When he had got it, he put it on the kitchen table beside Alfie, and even he could hardly tell that one was bigger than the other. But it *was* bigger. It was bigger by two ounces. This was Tortoise Number 2.

Mr Hoppy took Tortoise Number 2 out onto the balcony and gripped it in the claws of his tortoise-catcher. Then he lowered it onto Mrs Silver's balcony, right beside a nice fresh lettuce leaf.

Tortoise Number 2 had never eaten tender juicy lettuce leaves before. It had only had thick old cabbage leaves. It loved the lettuce and started chomping away at it with great gusto.

There followed a rather nervous two hours' wait for Mrs Silver to return from work.

Would she see any difference between the new tortoise and Alfie? It was going to be a tense moment.

Out onto her balcony swept Mrs Silver.

"Alfie, my darling!" she cried out. "Mummy's back! Have you missed me?"

Mr Hoppy, peering over his railing, but well hidden between two huge potted plants, held his breath.

The new tortoise was still chomping away at the lettuce.

"My my, Alfie, you do seem hungry today,"
Mrs Silver was saying. "It must be Mr Hoppy's
magic words I've been whispering to you."

Mr Hoppy watched as Mrs Silver picked the
tortoise up and stroked his shell. Then she
fished Mr Hoppy's piece of paper out of her
pocket, and holding the tortoise very close to
her face, she whispered, reading from the
paper:

"ESIO TROT, ESIO TROT,
TEG REGGIB REGGIB!
EMOC NO, ESIO TROT,
WORG PU, FFUP PU, TOOHS PU!
GNIRPS PU, WOLB PU, LLEWS PU!
EGROG! ELZZUG! FFUTS! PLUG!
TUP NO TAF, ESIO TROT, TUP NO TAF!
TEG NO, TEG NO! ELBBOG DOOF!"

Mr Hoppy popped his head out of the foliage and called out, "Good evening, Mrs Silver. How is Alfie tonight?"

"Oh, he's lovely," Mrs Silver said, looking up and beaming. "And he's developing *such* an appetite! I've never seen him eat like this before! It must be the magic words."

"You never know," Mr Hoppy said darkly. "You never know."

Mr Hoppy waited seven whole days before he made his next move.

On the afternoon of the seventh day, when Mrs Silver was at work, he lifted Tortoise Number 2 from the balcony below and brought it into his living room. Number 2 had weighed exactly *fifteen* ounces. He must now find one that weighed exactly *seventeen* ounces, two ounces more.

From his enormous collection, he easily found a seventeen-ounce tortoise and once again he made sure the shells matched in colour. Then he lowered Tortoise Number 3 onto Mrs Silver's balcony.

As you will have guessed by now, Mr Hoppy's secret was a very simple one. If a creature grows slowly enough – I mean very very slowly indeed – then you'll never notice that it has grown at all, especially if you see it every day.

It's the same with children. They are actually growing taller every week, but their mothers never notice it until they grow out of their clothes.

Slowly does it, Mr Hoppy told himself. Don't hurry it.

So this is how things went over the next eight weeks.

In the beginning

ALFIE   weight 13 ounces

End of first week

TORTOISE NO. 2   weight 15 ounces

End of second week

TORTOISE NO. 3   weight 17 ounces

44

End of third week

TORTOISE NO. 4   weight 19 ounces

End of fourth week

TORTOISE NO. 5   weight 21 ounces

End of fifth week

TORTOISE NO. 6   weight 23 ounces

TORTOISE NO. 7   weight 25 ounces

End of seventh week

TORTOISE NO. 8   weight 27 ounces

Alfie's weight was thirteen ounces. Tortoise Number 8 was twenty-seven ounces. Very slowly, over seven weeks, Mrs Silver's pet had more than doubled in size and the good lady hadn't noticed a thing.

Even to Mr Hoppy, peering down over his railing, Tortoise Number 8 looked pretty big. It was amazing that Mrs Silver had hardly noticed anything at all during the great operation. Only once had she looked up and said, "You know, Mr Hoppy, I do believe he's getting a bit bigger. What do you think?"

"I can't see a lot of difference myself," Mr Hoppy had answered casually.

But now perhaps it was time to call a halt, and that evening Mr Hoppy was just about to go out and suggest to Mrs Silver that she ought to weigh Alfie when a startled cry from the balcony below brought him outside fast.

"Look!" Mrs Silver was shouting. "Alfie's too big to get through the door of his little house! He must have grown enormously!"

"Weigh him," Mr Hoppy ordered. "Take him in and weigh him quick."

Mrs Silver did just that, and in half a minute she was back holding the tortoise in both hands and waving it above her head and shouting, "Guess what, Mr Hoppy! Guess what! He weighs twenty-seven ounces! He's twice as big as he was before! Oh you darling!" she cried, stroking the tortoise. "Oh, you great big wonderful boy! Just look what clever Mr Hoppy has done for you!"

Mr Hoppy suddenly felt very brave. "Mrs Silver," he said. "Do you think I could pop down to your balcony and hold Alfie myself?"

"Why, of course you can!" Mrs Silver cried. "Come down at once."

Mr Hoppy rushed down the stairs and Mrs Silver opened the door to him. Together they went out onto the balcony. "Just look at him!" Mrs Silver said proudly. "Isn't he grand!"

"He's a big good-sized tortoise now," Mr Hoppy said.

"And *you* did it!" Mrs Silver cried. "You're a miracle man, you are indeed!"

"But what *am* I going to do about his house?" Mrs Silver said. "He must have a house to go into at night, but now he can't get through the door."

They were standing on the balcony looking at the tortoise who was trying to push his way into his house. But he was too big.

"I shall have to enlarge the door," Mrs Silver said.

"Don't do that," Mr Hoppy said. "You mustn't go chopping up such a pretty little house. After all, he only needs to be just a tiny bit smaller and he could get in easily."

"How can he possibly get smaller?" Mrs Silver asked.

"That's simple," Mr Hoppy said. "Change the

magic words. Instead of telling him to get
bigger and bigger, tell him to get a bit smaller.
But in tortoise language of course."

"Will that work?"

"Of course it'll work."

"Tell me exactly what I have to say, Mr
Hoppy."

Mr Hoppy got out a piece of paper and a pencil and wrote:

ESIO TROT, ESIO TROT,
TEG A TIB RELLAMS, A TIB RELLAMS.

"That'll do it, Mrs Silver," he said, handing her the paper.

"I don't mind trying it," Mrs Silver said. "But look here, I wouldn't want him to get titchy small all over again, Mr Hoppy."

"He won't, dear lady, he won't," Mr Hoppy said. "Say it only tonight and tomorrow morning and then see what happens. We might be lucky."

"If it works," Mrs Silver said, touching him softly on the arm, "then you are the cleverest man alive."

The next afternoon, as soon as Mrs Silver had gone to work, Mr Hoppy lifted the tortoise up from her balcony and carried it inside. All he had to do now was to find one that was a shade smaller, so that it would just go through the door of the little house

He chose one and lowered it down with his tortoise-catcher. Then, still gripping the tortoise, he tested it to see if it would go through the door. It wouldn't.

He chose another. Again he tested it. This one went through nicely. Good. He placed the tortoise in the middle of the balcony beside a nice piece of lettuce and went inside to await Mrs Silver's homecoming.

That evening, Mr Hoppy was watering his plants on the balcony when suddenly he heard Mrs Silver's shouts from below, shrill with excitement.

"Mr Hoppy! Mr Hoppy! Where are you?" she was shouting. "Just look at this!"

Mr Hoppy popped his head over the railing and said, "What's up?"

"Oh, Mr Hoppy, it's worked!" she was crying. "Your magic words have worked again on Alfie! He can now get through the door of his little house! It's a miracle!"

"Can I come down and look?" Mr Hoppy shouted back.

"Come down at once, my dear man!" Mrs Silver answered. "Come down and see the wonders you have worked upon my darling Alfie!"

Mr
Hoppy
turned and
ran from the
balcony into the
living room, jumping
on tip toe like a ballet-
dancer between the sea of
tortoises that covered the floor.
He flung open his front door and
flew down the stairs two at a time with
the love songs of a thousand cupids ringing
in his ears. *This is it!* he whispered to himself
under his breath. *The greatest moment of my life is
coming up now! I mustn't bish it. I mustn't bosh it! I
must keep very calm!* When he was three-quarters
way down the stairs he caught sight of Mrs
Silver already standing at the open door waiting
to welcome him with a huge smile on her face.
She flung her arms around him and cried out,
"You really are the most wonderful man I've ever
met! You can do anything! Come in at once and
let me make you a cup of tea. That's the very
least you deserve!"

Seated in a comfortable armchair in Mrs
Silver's parlour, sipping his tea, Mr Hoppy was
all of a twitter. He looked at the lovely lady
sitting opposite him and smiled at her. She
smiled right back at him.

That smile of hers, so warm and friendly, suddenly gave him the courage he needed, and he said, "Mrs Silver, please will you marry me?"

"Why, Mr Hoppy!" she cried. "I didn't think you'd ever get round to asking me! Of course I'll marry you!"

Mr Hoppy got rid of his teacup and the two of them stood up and embraced warmly in the middle of the room.

"It's all due to Alfie," Mrs Silver said, slightly breathless.

"Good old Alfie," Mr Hoppy said. "We'll keep him for ever."

The next afternoon, Mr Hoppy took all his other tortoises back to the pet shops and said they could have them for nothing. Then he cleaned up his living room, leaving not a leaf of cabbage nor a trace of tortoise.

A few weeks later, Mrs Silver became Mrs Hoppy and the two of them lived very happily ever after.

P.S. I expect you are wondering what happened to little Alfie, the first of them all. Well, he was bought a week later from one of the pet shops by a small girl called Roberta Squibb, and he settled down in Roberta's garden. Every day she fed him lettuce and tomato slices and crispy celery, and in the winters he hibernated in a box of dried leaves in the tool shed.

That was a long time ago. Roberta has grown up and is now married and has two children of her own. She lives in another house, but Alfie is still with her, still the much-loved family pet, and Roberta reckons that by now he must be about thirty years old. It has taken him all that time to grow to twice the size he was when Mrs Silver had him. But he made it in the end.

TURN THE PAGE FOR A LOOK AT ANOTHER SCRUMDIDDLYUMPTIOUS STORY FROM ROALD DAHL!

Nᴏᴛ ꜰᴀʀ from where I live there is a queer old empty wooden house standing all by itself on the side of the road. I long to explore inside it but the door is always locked, and when I peer through a window all I can see is darkness and dust. I know the ground floor used once to be a shop because I can still read the faded lettering across the front which says ᴛʜᴇ ɢʀᴜʙʙᴇʀ. My mother has told me that in our part of the country in the olden days a grubber was another name for a sweet-shop, and now every time I look at it I think to myself what a lovely old sweet-shop it must have been.

On the shop-window itself somebody has painted in white the words ꜰᴏʀ ꜱᴀɪʟ.

One morning, I noticed that ꜰᴏʀ ꜱᴀɪʟ had been scraped off the shop-window and in its place some-body had painted ꜱᴏʟᴇᴅ. I stood there staring at the new writing and wishing like mad that it had been me who had bought it because then I would have been able to make it into a grubber all over again. I have always longed and longed to own a sweet-shop. The sweet-shop of my dreams would be loaded from top to bottom with Sherbet Suckers and Caramel Fudge and

Russian Toffee and Sugar Snorters and Butter Gum-
balls and thousands and thousands of other glorious
things like that. Oh boy, what I couldn't have done
with that old Grubber shop if it had been mine!

On my next visit to The Grubber, I was standing
across the road gazing at the wonderful old building
when suddenly an enormous bathtub came sailing out
through one of the second-floor windows and crashed
right on to the middle of the road!

A few moments later, a white porcelain lavatory pan with the wooden seat still on it came flying out of the same window and landed with a wonderful splintering crash just beside the bathtub. This was followed by a kitchen sink and an empty canary-cage and a four-poster bed and two hot-water bottles and a rocking horse and a sewing-machine and goodness knows what else besides.

It looked as though some madman was ripping out the whole of the inside of the house, because now pieces of staircase and bits of the banisters and a whole lot of old floorboards came whistling through the windows.

Then there was silence. I waited and waited but not another sound came from within the building. I crossed the road and stood right under the windows and called out, "Is anybody at home?"

There was no answer.

In the end it began to get dark so I had to turn away and start walking home. But you can bet your life nothing was going to stop me from hurrying back there again tomorrow morning to see what the next surprise was going to be.

When I got back to the Grubber house the next morning, the first thing I noticed was the new door. The dirty old brown door had been taken out and in its place someone had fitted a brand-new red one. The new door was fantastic. It was twice as high as the other one had been and it looked ridiculous. I couldn't begin to imagine who would want a tremendous tall door like that in his house unless it was a giant.

As well as this, somebody had scraped away the SOLED notice on the shop-window and now there was a whole lot of different writing all over the glass. I stood there reading it and reading it and trying to figure out what on earth it all meant.

The LWC Co

THE LADDERLESS
WINDOW·CLEANING
COMPANY ~
Get your windows
cleaned without
a lot of dirty
ladders leaning
against your
house.

I tried to catch some sign or sound of movement inside the house but there was none . . . until all of a sudden . . . out of the corner of my eye . . . I noticed that one of the windows on the top floor was slowly beginning to open outwards . . .

Then a HEAD appeared at the open window.

I stared at the head. The head stared back at me with big round dark eyes.

Suddenly, a second window was flung wide open and of all the crazy things a gigantic white bird hopped out and perched on the window-sill. I knew what this

one was because of its amazing beak which was shaped like a huge orange-coloured basin. The Pelican looked down at me and sang out:

> "Oh, how I wish
> For a big fat fish!
> I'm as hungry as ever could be!
> A dish of fish is my only wish!
> How far are we from the sea?"

"We are a long way from the sea," I called back to him, "but there is a fishmonger in the village not far away."

"A fish *what*?"

"A fish*monger*."

"Now what on earth would that be?" asked the Pelican. "I have heard of a fish-*pie* and a fish-*cake* and a fish-*finger*, but I have never heard of a fish-*monger*. Are these mongers good to eat?"

This question baffled me a bit, so I said, "Who is your friend in the next window?"

"She is the Giraffe!" the Pelican answered. "Is she not wonderful? Her legs are on the ground floor and her head is looking out of the top window!"

As if all this wasn't enough, the window on the *first floor* was now flung wide open and out popped a Monkey!

The Monkey stood on the window-sill and did a jiggly little dance. He was so skinny he seemed to be made only out of furry bits of wire, but he danced wonderfully well, and I clapped and cheered and did a little dance myself in return.

"We are the Window-Cleaners!" sang out the
Monkey.

> "We will polish your glass
> Till it's shining like brass
> And it sparkles like sun on the sea!
> We are quick and polite,
> We will come day or night,
> The Giraffe and the Pelly and me!
>
> We're a fabulous crew,
> We know just what to do,
> And we never stop work to drink tea.
> All your windows will glow
> When we give them a go,
> The Giraffe and the Pelly and me!
>
> We use water and soap
> Plus some kindness and hope,
> But we never use ladders, not we.
> Who needs ladders at all
> When you're thirty feet tall?
> Not Giraffe, and not Pelly! Not me!"

The Reader of Books

It's a funny thing about mothers and fathers. Even when their own child is the most disgusting little blister you could ever imagine, they still think that he or she is wonderful.

Some parents go further. They become so blinded by adoration they manage to convince themselves their child has qualities of genius.

Well, there is nothing very wrong with all this. It's the way of the world. It is only when the parents begin telling *us* about the brilliance of their own revolting offspring, that we start shouting, "Bring us a basin! We're going to be sick!"

School teachers suffer a good deal from having to listen to this sort of twaddle from proud parents, but they usually get their own back when the time comes to write the end-of-term reports. If I were a teacher I would cook up some real scorchers for the children of doting parents. "Your son Maximilian", I would write, "is a total wash-out. I hope you have a family business you can push him into when he leaves school because he sure as heck won't get a job anywhere else." Or if I were feeling lyrical that day, I might write, "It is a curious truth that grasshoppers have their hearing-organs in the sides of the abdomen. Your daughter Vanessa, judging by what she's learnt this term, has no hearing-organs at all."

I might even delve deeper into natural history and say, "The periodical cicada spends six years as a grub underground, and no more than six *days* as a free creature of sunlight and air. Your son Wilfred has spent six years as a grub in this school and we are still waiting for him to emerge from the chrysalis." A particularly poisonous little girl might sting me into saying, "Fiona has the same glacial beauty as an iceberg, but unlike the iceberg she has absolutely nothing below the surface." I

think I might enjoy writing end-of-term reports for the stinkers in my class. But enough of that. We have to get on.

Occasionally one comes across parents who take the opposite line, who show no interest at all in their children, and these of course are far worse than the doting ones. Mr and Mrs Wormwood were two such parents. They had a son called Michael and a daughter called Matilda, and the parents looked upon Matilda in particular as nothing more than a scab. A scab is something you have to put up with until the time comes when you can pick it off and flick it away. Mr and Mrs Wormwood looked forward enormously to the time when they could pick their little daughter off and flick her away, preferably into the next county or even further than that.

It is bad enough when parents treat *ordinary* children as though they were scabs and bunions, but it becomes somehow a lot worse when the child in question is *extra*ordinary, and by that I mean sensitive and brilliant. Matilda was both of these things, but above all she was brilliant. Her mind was so nimble and she was so quick to learn that her ability should have been obvious even to the most half-witted of parents. But Mr and Mrs Wormwood were both so gormless and so wrapped up in their own silly little lives that they failed to notice anything unusual about their daughter. To tell the truth, I doubt they would have noticed had she crawled into the house with a broken leg.

Matilda's brother Michael was a perfectly normal boy, but the sister, as I said, was something to make your eyes pop. By the age of *one and a half* her speech was perfect and she knew as many words as most grown-ups. The parents, instead of applauding her, called her a noisy chatterbox and told her sharply that small girls should be seen and not heard.

By the time she was *three*, Matilda had taught herself to read by studying newspapers and magazines that lay around the house. At the age of *four*, she could read fast and well and she naturally began hankering after books. The only book in the whole of this enlightened household was something called *Easy Cooking* belonging to her mother, and when she had read this from cover to cover and had learnt all the recipes by heart, she decided she wanted something more interesting.

"Daddy," she said, "do you think you could buy me a book?"

"A *book*?" he said. "What d'you want a flaming book for?"

"To read, Daddy."

"What's wrong with the telly, for heaven's sake? We've got a lovely telly with a twelve-inch screen and now you come asking for a book! You're getting spoiled, my girl!"

Nearly every weekday afternoon Matilda was left alone in the house. Her brother (five years older than her) went to school. Her father went to work and her mother went out playing bingo in a town eight miles away. Mrs Wormwood was hooked on bingo and played it five afternoons a week. On the afternoon of the day when her father had refused to buy her a book, Matilda set out all by herself to walk to the public library in the village. When she arrived, she introduced herself to the librarian, Mrs Phelps. She asked if she might sit awhile and read a book. Mrs Phelps, slightly taken aback at the arrival of such a tiny girl unacccompanied by a parent, nevertheless told her she was very welcome.

"Where are the children's books please?" Matilda asked.

"They're over there on those lower shelves," Mrs Phelps told her. "Would you like me to help you find a nice one with lots of pictures in it?"

"No, thank you," Matilda said. "I'm sure I can manage."

From then on, every afternoon, as soon as her mother had left for bingo, Matilda would toddle down to the library. The walk took only ten minutes and this allowed her two glorious hours sitting quietly by herself in a cosy corner devouring one book after another. When she had read every single children's book in the place, she started wandering round in search of something else.

Mrs Phelps, who had been watching her with fascination for the past few weeks, now got up from her desk and went over to her. "Can I help you, Matilda?" she asked.

"I'm wondering what to read next," Matilda said. "I've finished all the children's books."

"You mean you've looked at the pictures?"

"Yes, but I've read the books as well."

Mrs Phelps looked down at Matilda from her great height and Matilda looked right back up at her.

"I thought some were very poor," Matilda said, "but others were lovely. I liked *The Secret Garden* best of all. It was full of mystery. The mystery of

the room behind the closed door and the mystery of the garden behind the big wall."

Mrs Phelps was stunned. "Exactly how old are you, Matilda?" she asked.

"Four years and three months," Matilda said.

Mrs Phelps was more stunned than ever, but she had the sense not to show it. "What sort of a book would you like to read next?" she asked.

Matilda said, "I would like a really good one that grown-ups read. A famous one. I don't know any names."

Mrs Phelps looked along the shelves, taking her time. She didn't quite know what to bring out. How, she asked herself, does one choose a famous grown-up book for a four-year-old girl? Her first thought was to pick a young teenager's romance of the kind that is written for fifteen-year-old schoolgirls, but for some reason she found herself instinctively walking past that particular shelf.

"Try this," she said at last. "It's very famous and very good. If it's too long for you, just let me know and I'll find something shorter and a bit easier."

"*Great Expectations*," Matilda read, "by Charles Dickens. I'd love to try it."

I must be mad, Mrs Phelps told herself, but to Matilda she said, "Of course you may try it."

Over the next few afternoons Mrs Phelps could hardly take her eyes from the small girl sitting for hour after hour in the big armchair at the far end of the room with the book on her lap. It was necessary to rest it on the lap because it was too heavy for her to hold up, which meant she had to sit leaning forward in order to read. And a strange sight it was, this tiny dark-haired person sitting there with her feet nowhere near touching the floor, totally absorbed in the wonderful adventures of Pip and old Miss Havisham and her cobwebbed house and by the spell of magic that Dickens the great story-teller had woven with his words. The only movement from the reader was the lifting of the hand every now and then to turn over a page, and Mrs Phelps always felt sad when the time came for her to cross the floor and say, "It's ten to five, Matilda."

During the first week of Matilda's visits Mrs Phelps had said to her, "Does your mother walk you down here every day and then take you home?"

"My mother goes to Aylesbury every afternoon to play bingo," Matilda had said. "She doesn't know I come here."

"But that's surely not right," Mrs Phelps said. "I think you'd better ask her."

"I'd rather not," Matilda said. "She doesn't encourage reading books. Nor does my father."

"But what do they expect you to do every afternoon in an empty house?"

"Just mooch around and watch the telly."

"I see."

"She doesn't really care what I do," Matilda said a little sadly.

Mrs Phelps was concerned about the child's safety on the walk through the fairly busy village High Street and the crossing of the road, but she decided not to interfere.